Oscar's Half Birthday

BOB GRAHAM

WALKER BOOKS
AND SUBSIDIARIES
LONDON · BOSTON · SYDNEY · AUCKLAND

"Perfect day for half a birthday,"
says Oscar's dad.

The birthday boy waves his wet fists.

"And a picnic," says Oscar's mum.

Boris the dog raises one ear.

"With a birthday cake," says Oscar's sister, Millie.

She wears coat-hanger fairy wings
on her back and a dinosaur glove on her hand.
She's excited, and the dinosaur squeezes
Oscar's arm into soft little pillows.

"Careful, Millie," says Mum.

"A little more fairy and not so much
dinosaur," says Dad.

"But he's so CUTE," says Millie.

"I know," says Dad, and wraps
three tuna sandwiches in plastic.

scar's birthday.

ly his birthday –

months old.

is, no one can

whole birthday...

"Dinosaurs and fairies"
For our Rosie, who knows about these things

First published 2005 by Walker Books Ltd, 87 Vauxhall Walk, London SE11 5HJ

This edition published 2008

10 9 8 7 6 5 4 3 2

This book has been typeset in StempelSchneidler.

Printed in China

British Library Cataloguing in Publication Data: a catalogue record for this book is available from the British Library

ISBN 978-1-4063-0686-6

www.walker.co.uk

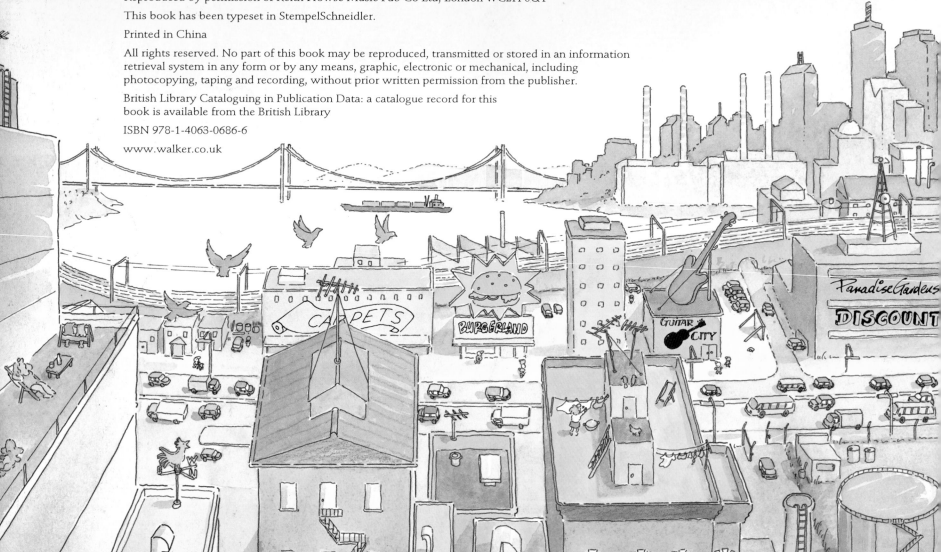

"Where are we going?" asks Millie.

"The country," replies Dad.

"Well, not really the country," says Mum,

"up on Bellevue Hill."

"Half the country then," says Dad.

"For half a birthday," adds Mum.

In the lift, Millie the dinosaur presses all the buttons.

Bright as a Christmas tree they shine,

bright as candles on a cake,

glinting in Oscar's dark eyes…

They are a long time getting to the street.

They walk past the gasworks,
along by the factory gate
and across the footbridge.

High up over the traffic,

Oscar kicks his feet in the wind.

Millie's wings flap as Mum holds her tight.

Seagulls screech and bank off towards

the docks on the other side of the city.

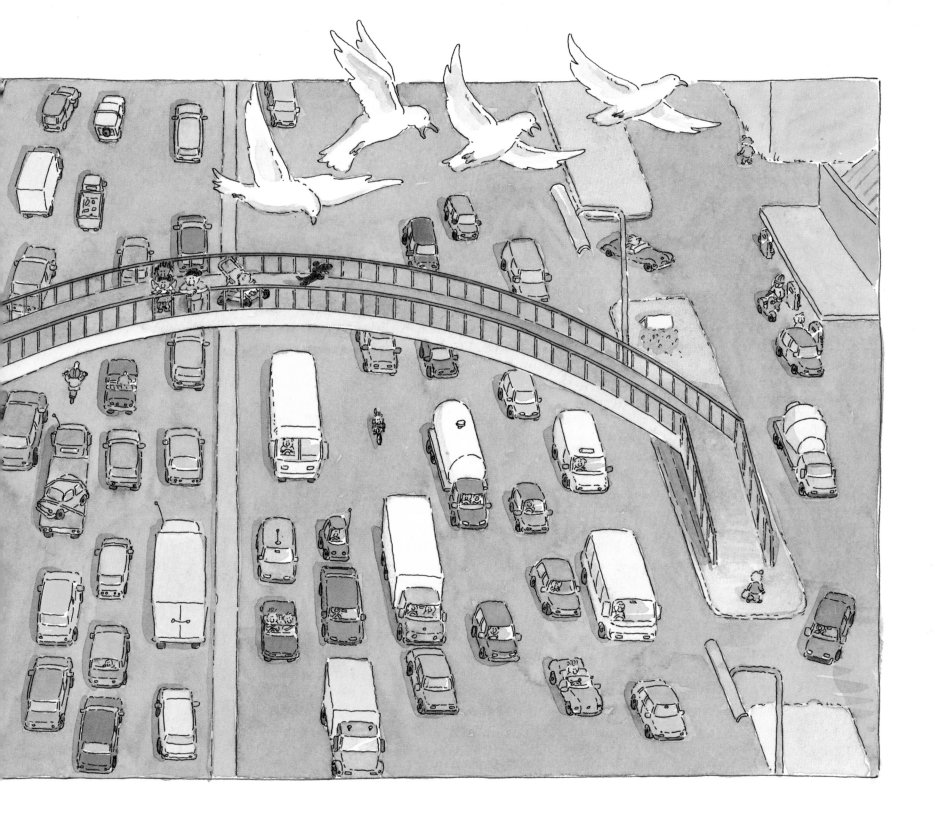

They push the pram slowly along by the canal,

wheels squeaking, Oscar waving, and stop in the tunnel.

There is a rushing of wind.

"HERE SHE COMES!" yells Dad.

Tickety-clack, tickety-clack, tickety-clack.

The eleven fifteen is belting down the track so fast

Millie can feel it all the way up through her pink sneakers.

"AND THERE SHE GOES!" yells Millie.

Tickety-clack, tickety-clack, tickety-clack –

fading away until all that can be

heard is the echo of water

dripping off the bridge,

plip, plip, plip,

into the canal below.

And at last they reach Bellevue Hill.

"Can we have our picnic now?" Millie asks.

"Well, let's find a nice spot first," says Mum.

"Are you hungry already?" says Dad.

"Yes," replies Millie.

"That's the dinosaur talking," says Mum.

"Not the fairy," adds Dad.

Millie the dinosaur grazes on
grass seeds stripped from their stalks
and Oscar falls quietly asleep
with his mouth open,
as they push on up the hill.

Near the top, the path goes through woods.

They listen to the wind in the trees

and the drone of distant traffic.

Boris chases rabbits.

Oscar frowns up against the light –

six different expressions on his face

in the time it takes a leaf to fall.

Out of the woods,

there is sunshine all around.

"There's our picnic spot!" Mum points.

"It's just waiting for us."

It seems the whole town is up here

this afternoon, all admiring Oscar.

"Oh, he's GORGEOUS!"

"What a sweetie!"

"Cute little smile."

"Eyes like his mum's."

"Has his dad's nose."

"He's my brother," says Millie.

"He's an angel!" says somebody. "Should have wings like his sister."

Oscar sits on the picnic rug swaying like a tightrope walker, trying to keep his balance.

"I can't wait. Let's do it now," says Mum.

She has a chocolate cake
she made specially,
with half a candle on top.

"Yes, light it, Mummy," says Millie.

Mum ducks behind a tree, cups her hands against the wind,

and the little half candle flickers to life.

"HAAAAAAAAPY..." she begins.

A voice joins in from across the grass.

And another. And another.

"HAPPY BIRTHDAY TO YOU!" they sing.

More people join in.

"HAPPY BIRTHDAY TO YOU!"

Now the whole hillside is singing.

"HAPPY BIRTHDAY, DEAR..."

"What's your name, my young friend?"
asks a man.

"Oscar," replies Millie.

"OSCAR!

HAPPY BIRTHDAY TO YOU!"

The wind whips their song up over the hill, out across the traffic,

high over churches and factories and apartment buildings.

Its sound falls gently over the city – so faint and thin,

only dogs can hear it.

And somewhere down there,

the one who started all of this …

the half-birthday boy, OSCAR,

sits tilted at an angle, his fingers

curled into Millie's tuna sandwich.

His shoulders are hunched,

his head nods

and the sun shines through

his ears, lighting them up

like little lanterns.

The song finishes and there is silence. "Thank you," Mum calls, dabbing at a tear on her cheek. "He's too young to blow the candle out – anyway the wind has already done that."

There is a smattering of applause and the family takes a bow, as Oscar at last topples sideways into Boris's Happy Snappys.

Boris makes short work of his picnic.

In the evening,
as lights come on all over the city,
a forest of night lights burns in the
soap dish for Oscar's half birthday.

"Oh, I haven't given him a present,"
says Millie. "Here, Oscar, you can
have a turn with my dinosaur."
The dinosaur goes straight into
Oscar's mouth.
"Look, a baby eating a dinosaur!"
says Mum.
"I think he's getting teeth," says Dad.

After dinner, Mum and Dad clear a space and dance.

Dad hums along (a little out of tune) to the music

as they dip and sway,

circle and glide …

like two boats on a calm night sea.

As the music ends, Dad lowers Mum slowly

backwards to the floor where she lands with a soft bump.

Only Boris's tail plays on,

thump, thump, thump,

like a drummer off the beat.

Oscar is already asleep.

Millie gently takes her dinosaur away from him.

No use wasting it on a sleeping half-year-old baby, is there?

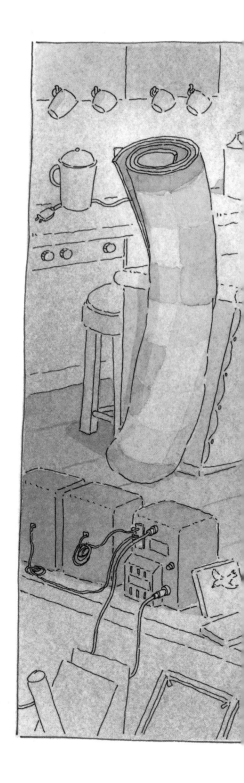

"Whose birthday is next?" asks Millie.

"Yours, with four full candles on the cake," replies Mum.

"Mine!" murmurs Millie, and she falls asleep too,

her coat-hanger fairy wings

still attached.